For John Thacher Hurd

When he comes

(He's here)

ISBN 0-439-38845-7

12 11 10 9 8 7 6 5 4 3 2 1   2 3 4 5 6 7/0

Printed in Mexico   49

First Scholastic printing, January 2002

My book. Mother's book.
In my book I only look.

The fire burns.

The pages turn.

Mother's chair.
My chair.
   A low chair.
   A high chair.
   But certainly my chair.

Daddy's slippers.
My slippers.
My pajamas.
Daddy's pajamas.
Even my teddy bear
Wears pajamas.

My dog.
Daddy's dog.
Daddy's dog
Once caught a frog.

My spoon.
Daddy's spoon.
"The moon belongs
   To the man in the moon."

Daddy's boy.
Mother's boy.
My boy is just a toy
Bear.

My car.
Daddy's car.

Bang Bang Bang—My car.

My car won't go very far.

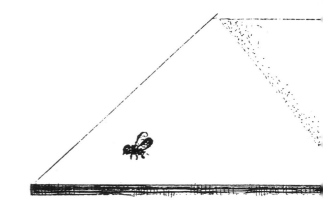

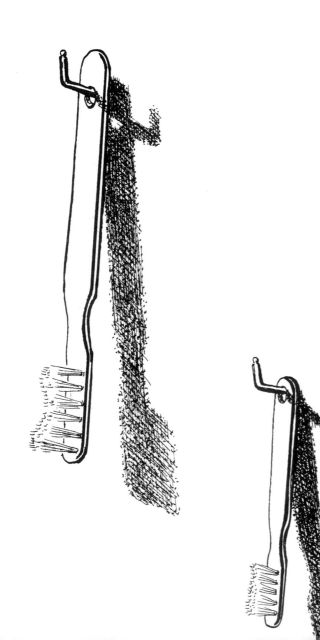

My toothbrush.
Daddy's toothbrush.

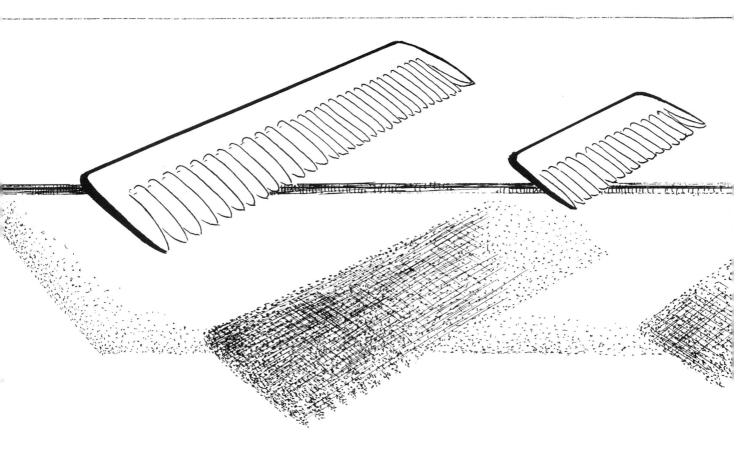

My comb.
Mother's comb.

My soap. Daddy's soap.

My soap will make soapsuds, I hope.

My fish.
Daddy's fish.
When you catch
A fish you make
A wish.

My bed.
Mother's bed.
I go to sleep
When my story is read,
When my prayers are said,
And when my head
Is sleepy on the pillow.

My breakfast.
My morning.
Daddy's breakfast.
Good morning.

My kitty.
Daddy's kitty.
Daddy's kitty
Has gone to the city.

Your world.
My world.

I can swing
Right over the world.

My tree.

The bird's tree.